I0788388

To the children who call me Mum,
the children I have taught,
and the children I am yet to meet.

You are loved, you belong and you are enough.

This book is for you.

The Week Our Teacher Escaped
Written By: Peta Ogilvie
Illustrated By: Ingrid Orlando Zon
Decorative Page By: Peta Ogilvie

First published and printed, 2025

Published by Little Kookaburra Creative, WA, Australia
www.littlekcreative.com

A catalogue record for this book is available from the National Library of Australia.

ISBN 978-1-7641387-0-3 (Hardcover)
ISBN 978-1-7641387-1-0 (Paperback)
ISBN 978-1-7641387-2-7 (Ebook)

The Week Our Teacher Escaped!

Written By: Peta Ogilvie

Illustrated By: Ingrid Orlando Zon

I thought I saw my teacher down the street the other day.

Could it **really** have been her, walking the other way?

I **WONDERED** what my teacher
did when I was not at school.

Did she sleep inside the classroom?

Now wouldn't that be cool?

snoooooze
pfffff
whiff
zzz

Did she have a **bed** and **bathroom**
in one of the storerooms?
SWOOSH!
BANG!

But how would she fit in there,
with all the books and brooms?

Did she have a **magic** kitchen, underneath the sink?

But how would she **fit** in there, with all the stamps and ink?

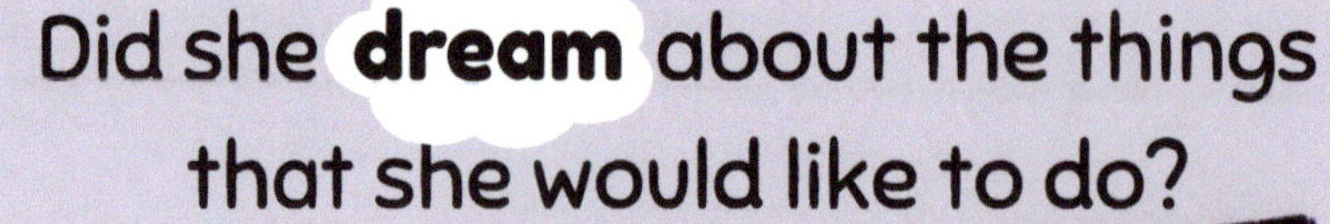

Did she **dream** about the things
that she would like to do?

Like SEEING all the monkeys
and meerkats at the zoo.

Did she **SIT** down on the mat,
or at my blue desk chair?

How strange her life **MUST** be,
spending all her time in there.

Or maybe she just vanished,
'til the morning bell rang loud.

A secret life of mystery,
that teachers aren't allowed!

I went and asked my classmates –
They wondered the same thing too!

"Let's **investigate**!" we said,
"Yes, that's what we **will** do!"

On Monday morning, May announced,
she got a SHOCK that made her STOP.

She saw our teacher with a trolley,
in the grocery shop!

On Tuesday, Ted told us she was topping up her car!

On Wednesday, Wes reported,
she was at the movie candy bar!

On Thursday, Theo saw her eating eggs in a café.

On Friday, Frankie found her
snorkelling 'round the bay.

On Saturday, Sam saw her spectating at kids' sport!

On Sunday, Seb stated,
she was strolling by the court.

Wait!...
What?
Hang on a minute!
The movies, the shop, the fuel?

We always thought our teacher
lived each day at school!

The café, the sports, the bay,
and **even** walking by the courts.

"How can this be true?" we said,
but we'd heard all the reports!

We put our heads together,
and we ALL had to agree,
that our teacher was a HUMAN.
The same as you and me!